Conned

Christine Bell

Entangled Publishing, LLC
2614 South Timberline Road
Suite 109
Fort Collins, CO 80525
Visit our website at www.entangledpublishing.com.

Brazen is an imprint of Entangled Publishing, LLC. For more information on our titles, visit www.brazenbooks.com.

Edited by Kerri-Leigh Grady and Allison Blisard
Cover design by Heather Howland
Photography by Thinkstock

Manufactured in the United States of America

First Edition November 2013

For my husband Chip. What I saw was what I got. You are everything you seemed and so much more. I love you every single day.

Chapter One

"Oh my God. Oh, God. *Yeah*. Yeah, right there. Yes. Yes!"

For the first half a minute, Professor Tucker Lamb had tried to muscle through, but the sounds coming from the adjacent classroom had escalated and were now too distracting to ignore. His inseam was feeling decidedly shorter than it had a minute ago, and his students couldn't mask their reactions any longer.

Most of the girls wrinkled their noses and laughed softly to one another, leaning across the aisles between the rows of silver desks. Some of the guys tried to follow suit, but their halfhearted attempts came off as wooden. They couldn't hide their fascination or their extreme interest in finding out who was behind the very vocal "O" coming through the wall.

Tuck knew exactly who was responsible. Fortunately, his students were freshmen, so most probably hadn't met the Human Sexuality professor, Dr. Eleanor Malloy. And it was a good thing because if they had, there would have been a stampede to get out of his classroom and into hers.

She didn't look like any "Eleanor" he'd ever seen and went by Cricket instead. When they'd got to talking at the staff Christmas party last year, she'd explained that her dad had given her the nickname when she was a child because she never liked to sleep. She made noise all night long. He had to bite his tongue to keep from asking her if that was still the case and if she'd give him a shot to be the guy behind all the noise.

"Okay, guys. It sounds like Dr. Malloy's lesson is winding down now, so let's try to focus," he said with a smile he hoped didn't look as pained as it felt.

He wondered how many times she'd been slapped on the wrist for her outrageous classroom antics. Still, she was well known for making the material relatable and easy to understand, so the students loved her. Moreover, he respected her because she practiced what she preached. She defended her subject of expertise like a wolverine and was very vocal about her view of human sexuality as an integral part of life. There was nothing dirty or tawdry about it, thank you very much. Her attitude came through in her teaching, and no subject was taboo. She was fearless, and he admired that.

But that fearlessness came with a price. In Cricket's case, it made her a target for the school's administrators. Tuck suspected that her appearance did little to help her case. Five foot nothing, a hundred and thirty-five pounds comprised almost entirely of tits and ass, she was like something from a tractor-trailer's mud flap. A sailor's bawdy tattoo. Or a science professor's wet dream.

She was hell on wheels and exactly the kind of woman he would have gone for before…

"I think I want to change majors," one of the kids in the back row said, dragging him back to reality.

The other students chuckled, some nodding their agreement.

"Hey, hey. Science can be just as fun as human sexuality," Tuck protested.

"Yeah, right. Even you don't believe that, Prof."

True that.

"Seriously. The two subjects actually go hand in hand in a lot of ways. For instance, attraction, or what people refer to as 'chemistry'? Those are measurable physical manifestations of hormones in your bodies. That's all science."

His class seemed riveted now, and he continued, their enthusiasm fueling his. "You wouldn't even feel that attraction if it weren't for those natural chemicals running through your bloodstream. Then neurotransmitters take the wheel and start firing all over the place. Adrenaline pounds through your veins from the rush. Dopamine and serotonin flood in from all the pleasure. Oxytocin is released as you complete the"—he cleared his throat—"act."

Again, his students laughed.

"Then finally vasopressin sneaks in, making you want to snuggle and maybe stick around for the long haul."

"I don't think I have any of the last kind," one of the boys in the front row deadpanned to another round of chuckles.

"Maybe you just suppress yours, Baxter. Okay," Tuck continued, enamored with the topic as the kernel of an idea formed. "I'm liking the track we're on, and it's clear you guys are more interested in this discussion than any we've had so far, so let's explore those connections in a deeper way. As you all know, the syllabus calls for a research paper next month."

He put up a hand to silence the chorus of groans.

"I know, I know, so here's what we'll do. Let's make it a research *project* instead. A project that will help us explore the relationship between science and human sexuality." And more importantly, help him explore a relationship between him and Dr. Cricket Malloy. It was asking for trouble, but now that the thought had wormed its way in, there was no stopping it. "If you still want to do a paper, go for it. If not, use your imagination. You can do a PowerPoint presentation, charts and graphs, create a survey or a video."

Snickers swept the room, and he rolled his eyes.

"Not *that* kind of video. I mean a video chronicling your research. I'll allow you to work in groups if you'd like, no more than three members per group so we still get a wide variety of topics and mediums. You'll have three weeks to work on your projects and then we'll spend the fourth week on presenting them to the class so we can all benefit from one another's efforts." He smiled at them and spread his arms wide. "This time next month, we'll all be enlightened."

The students chattered excitedly about their new assignment. While over the past six months he'd managed to build a reputation as a "nice" professor, he wasn't on the short list of "cool" ones, so they were clearly all amped about this turn of events.

"Each group should come to our next class with three possible ideas for my approval, and we'll go from there."

As the students talked, Tuck's thoughts flipped again to the doctor in the next room. Now that he was out of that life and on the up and up, she was exactly the kind of woman he needed to steer clear of. The kind of woman who stuck in deep and wouldn't let go, like a barbed hook in a trout's gullet. And after ten long years of struggling, he'd finally become a man he could be proud of, and he needed some time to settle into it. To make sure it stuck. Not to mention, they were coworkers. Nothing like stirring up some uncomfortable workplace drama if and when things didn't work out when he was just finally feeling at home here.

But, *damn*.

She was driving him bananas. Absolutely fucking crazy. Aside from a couple impromptu lunches when they ran into each other in the professors' lounge, he rarely saw her for more than a passing hello, but every time he did, he had to avert his eyes. It was that or walk around campus sporting a massive boner. Not okay. But he'd managed to avoid making a play at her because most of the time she was out of sight, if not totally out of mind. Now, though, with her right in his face day in, day out? It was nearly impossible to stop thinking about her.

Totally wrong for you. Stop this before you even start.

In spite of every instinct warning him off, the prospect of getting close to Cricket Malloy sent a familiar surge of power thrumming in his blood. The riot of heady sensations assailed him, pulling at him, urging him to get closer to the forbidden prize…sensations he hadn't felt since the last time he was on the grift.

A plan came into sharp focus. And damn, it felt good.

• • •

Cricket splashed some Irish creamer into her coffee and gave it a stir. Today's lesson had been a fun one. The students had really seemed to get it, too, which was always validating. After two years she felt at home at Westfield and, for the first time in her adult life, thought she might want to stay in one place for a while.

"Hello there, Dr. Malloy, welcome to Adams Hall."

She turned to see Professor Tucker Lamb stroll into the staff lounge area. "Hello, yourself. And thanks for the welcome." She glanced around at the sparsely furnished room. Three square tables were lined up in a neat row, each fitted out with utilitarian, dark wood chairs. If she was going to be here for more than a week, she'd have to bring in some colorful tablecloths and a vase filled with flowers to add some cheer to the seventeenth-century Puritan chic. "It's not the same as home, but it beats the hell out of getting stung to death."

The Facilities Department had cordoned off the Psych building that housed her classroom while a crew of exterminators dealt with an infestation of hornets. The department was scattered throughout the campus now, set up in every available classroom until they got the all-clear. She'd lucked out, landing herself the last room in the Math and Science building.

"Agreed," he said with a warm smile.

A little over six feet tall, with sandy hair and nice hazel eyes, he was pretty cute. With any effort, he could have had the better part of the school's female population, students and teachers alike, wrapped around his finger. But he seemed entirely unaware of his appearance and was pretty much all business, so the initial response to his looks wore off fast. Instead of campus hottie, he was known as a good, solid professor. Polite, but reserved. Almost shy.

She eyed him speculatively and wondered if he ever let loose, took off the tie, and maybe used it on a pretty woman's wrists. God, he'd probably be mortified by that thought. She could almost picture his face flushing with embarrassment.

Despite her lascivious thoughts, she vowed to be on her best behavior and not tease him. He wasn't her type, anyway. She didn't like jerks, but she did like 'em bad. Not "cheat on a woman with her sister" or "steal her life's savings" bad. More like "spank her ass" or "ride a Harley" bad. It was a real shame that bad boys also seemed to be bad boyfriends long-term.

"Death by bees is not on my top ten list of ways to go." He cleared his throat. "So, we, ah, heard your lesson today…" He trailed off, shifting his gaze away from hers.

She smothered a chuckle at his obvious discomfort and put him out of his misery. "Oh, that wasn't me. I was giving a lesson on the psychology of the fake orgasm. I rolled out the DVD of *When Harry Met Sally*…and let Meg Ryan help me with the last part. That scene is classic and the boys' faces were priceless. Up until that moment, I think they honestly believed they'd never had a girl fake it with them."

His cheeks did flush then, but he gave her a polite smile anyway. The devil in her smacked down the angel, who had just convinced her to be good. "Did you know studies show that eighty percent of women have faked orgasm? And fifty percent admit to doing it on a regular basis?"

"I, uh, I did not know that. Interesting." He pulled up a chair and eased his long frame into it. "And the psychology behind it?" He leaned in, as if he was truly interested in her answer.

She warmed to her subject quickly. "Surprisingly, or maybe not, a woman's need to nurture often comes into play. She doesn't want to hurt her man's pride. Then again, sometimes it's just that she wants to get it over with. Maybe she's tired but didn't want to disappoint her lover by saying no. There are a lot of different reasons." She shrugged. "Suffice it to say, it happens. A lot."

"And what about you, Professor?" He snagged her gaze with his own and a jolt ran through her. "Do you think those are valid reasons?"

For a second, she wondered if he was flirting with her. If so, he was better at it than she would've thought. Why hadn't she ever noticed how downright soulful his hazel eyes were? Probably because he'd never looked directly at her before. He'd always seemed a little hesitant. Nervous, even. He sure didn't look nervous now. *Very interesting.*

She took a long sip of her coffee before responding, but that damned devil took hold of her tongue once again. "I don't think there *is* a valid reason. And, in case you were wondering, I don't fake it." She lifted her chin and stared him down. "Ever."

He didn't break eye contact this time though, and she swore she saw something in his face. Not embarrassment, but something hot. She looked harder, and it was gone.

He sat back with an affable grin. "Yes, well, it does seem counterproductive. And you're a smart lady, so it stands to reason that you wouldn't."

She'd wondered if he would take the bait, but he'd chosen to retreat instead. It was kind of a letdown, but kind of cute at the same time. He was a bit of a puzzle, and damn if that didn't have her heart kicking up a notch.

She almost laughed out loud at her own reaction. She knew a sign when she saw one, and if a nerdy professor *not* flirting with her was getting her all hot and bothered, she had obviously gone without a man for too long.

Mentally, she started to calculate the months and was on eleven when Tucker spoke again.

"Actually, I'm glad I ran into you. I have a proposition," he said.

Her eyes snapped back to his. Maybe he was going to surprise her after all.

"Do you have any wiggle room in your syllabus?"

Okay, so maybe not.

"Depends."

"Your lesson got my students talking. They were so animated and engaged for the first time this semester. I felt like I needed to seize the opportunity to have a real moment with them." He scrubbed at the beginnings of five o'clock bristle on his chin absently. "I've challenged them to do a project on the correlation between human sexuality and science. I wanted them to see that science is a huge field and can be applied to almost any discipline. They were so enthralled by what was going on in your classroom, I figured what better way to make my point than with a topic they're so enthusiastic about."

A tickle of excitement at the idea of a fresh, new project ran through her. This was her favorite part of teaching. "I'm intrigued."

"I was thinking maybe we could do companion lessons. So your class could do the same type of project. Then we could get the classes together to share presentations and see how the classes differ in their approaches, do some cross-pollination, so to speak. What do you say?"

She took a deep sip of her coffee as she mulled over his

proposition. It could be a great experience for the students. And if she was being totally honest with herself, she had to admit she was more intrigued by Tucker Lamb with every passing minute. It couldn't hurt to spend some time around a nice guy for a change, could it?

Oh, what the hell.

"It sounds like fun, and both classes will probably learn something new and different. I'm in."

It did sound fun, and she was always down to shake things up a little. And along the vein of shaking things up a little…

"Hey, maybe we should do one, too. A project, I mean."

He stared at her for a second, nonplussed.

She tried to keep a straight face as she continued. "We'll do one together. To present to the kids. Show 'em how it's done. What about…myths and truths of aphrodisiacs? I've always been fascinated with them, truth be told, and it could be really interesting."

"What—" He paused and cleared his throat. "What would our research consist of?"

She was definitely getting to him now. The pulse in his neck beat strong, and she quelled the urge to close her teeth over that spot.

Oh yeah, way too long.

"We could set up controlled experiments in the science lab using stimuli purported to create or increase sexual arousal. Sounds, tastes, smells, and so on. We'll measure deviations in pupil dilation, vitals, and other data, depending on what equipment we can wrangle up. Obviously, we won't tell the students who the test subjects were," she said with a chuckle. "That would only start tongues a-wagging. But even at that, they'll get a kick out of the results. And don't worry, we'll keep it very scientific so as not to offend your modesty." She shot him a grin. "So, what do *you* say?"

She wet her lips as a bout of nerves set her stomach jiggling. His hazel eyes had darkened to the color of a stormy summer sky, and the sudden heat they gave off settled in the cradle of her thighs.

Tucker stared at her mouth for a long moment before responding.

"Yes. I say yes."

Chapter Two

Two days later, Tuck stood in the shower, still contemplating the strange workings of fate.

He couldn't believe his luck. He'd wanted more time with Cricket but never dreamed it would be so easy. And even better, she'd done the work *for* him. He hadn't even needed to broach the subject. Talk about great minds thinking alike.

He bent low, letting the steamy water sluice over his head and down his back. When he'd thought to include her and her class in the lesson, he was just hoping to go on a few lesson-planning dates with her. He'd never even dreamed they'd be doing hands-on research. Using aphrodisiacs, no less. It was so suggestive, so rife with possibilities.

Had that been her intention? He didn't even know anymore. One second she teased; the next, she seemed to actually be flirting with him. Her view on sexuality was so matter-of-fact, she could just be looking at this as a viable and interesting research project. But what if she wasn't?

He needed to figure out where her head was so he played it just right. If this was an opportunity to see her naked and he missed it, he'd find the nearest building and jump. On the flip side, he didn't want to make a jackass of himself if it turned out she was only trying to be friendly.

Because friendly didn't even scratch the surface of what he was feeling.

Maybe getting tangled up with her would be okay if she were just a regular girl. Pretty, nice, bright, someone to settle down with. Someone who would be content going to nice restaurants, ice skating, and maybe playing bridge on the weekends.

But that wasn't him, and it sure as hell wasn't Cricket. Her intellect was as sharp as her humor. And while she seemed kind, he didn't think of her as nice. He didn't want to take her to fancy restaurants, either. He wanted to make her dinner at home and suck her finger as she fed him until she begged him to bend her over the table and fuck her. He wanted to ski black diamonds with her, then race back to the outdoor hot tub and have mind-blowing sex outside where someone might or might not hear them. And if they played cards, he wanted it to be strip poker, where they'd both cheat to win if they had to.

For a long-term relationship to work, didn't someone need to be the voice of reason? The rock in the storm?

Tuck scrubbed a hand over his face in frustration. No matter what his brain was trying to tell him, the reality was that she set him off. All thrusters engaged.

It didn't help matters that she was practically made for pleasure. Her body with its dips and curves and all that soft flesh. Her lips, so full, so juicy. He wanted to take the bottom one between his teeth and suck…then press her to her knees and have her wrap that mouth around his length, working him up and down.

His cock twitched in enthusiastic agreement. The thought of her made him wild inside, like he was an addict and she was his fix. He'd felt that need before in his life, and he knew one thing for sure: needing something that bad was never good.

Tuck closed his eyes and tried to picture his high school football defensive coordinator, Coach Abba. They'd called him Abba the Hutt, and just thinking of him was usually enough to take the edge off all but the heartiest of boners.

No dice this time, though. In one hour, he was expected to be at the lab, where he would spend the better part of his afternoon testing out aphrodisiacs with the sexiest woman on the planet. He wondered briefly if anyone had ever died of horniness. He looked down at his swollen cock and let out a disgusted snort. Maybe it wouldn't kill him, but if he didn't take care of it, he definitely wouldn't be able to walk straight.

Tuck grabbed hold of the cheeky fucker and squeezed, shutting out his confusion, tuning out the noise in his head, and allowing himself to just feel. He groaned as he gripped his shaft, rubbing the distended head hard on the upstroke.

The memory of Cricket rushed in like an all-encompassing wave. Her citrus smell, the golden silk of her skin, the long, tawny hair, the cleavage that beckoned him to slide his cock between those breasts until he exploded on her chest.

Fantasy replaced memory. Her curvy hips clutched in his hands as she rode him hard. She'd lean forward so he could take one dusky nipple deep into his mouth and suck, while her tight pussy slid over him again and again.

Heat pooled low in his groin as he fine-tuned the picture on his HD, mind's-eye screen. Cricket's teeth closing over her bottom lip as she struggled not to cry out. Her gorgeous tits bouncing as she fucked him, faster and faster. Her greedy hand slipping between them, rubbing her clit in quick strokes.

His stomach muscles clenched. He could almost hear her breath coming in pants as she whimpered his name.

"Tucker, oh God, yeah."

He groaned in response, his leg muscles quivering as the pressure built, sensation overloading his brain. He worked himself harder, blood roaring in his ears as his balls tightened, ready to blow.

The climax hit him like a wrecking ball, smashing through his fantasy, splintering it into pure, incoherent pleasure. He came hard, hot liquid pumping out in spurts as shudders ripped through him.

Gasping for air, he put a steadying hand on the slippery tile and waited for his heart to stop pounding.

He stayed like that until the water cooled, drawing him back to reality.

Damn.

This wasn't the first time he'd come while thinking about Cricket Malloy. Shit, it wasn't even the tenth. But it had never seemed so real before.

Maybe because, for the first time ever, the things he'd imagined were actually possible.

Tuck groaned as his just-sated cock pulsed back to life. If just *thinking* about her made him feel like this, what would it be like having sex with her? He didn't know if he'd live through it.

And worse? He didn't know if he cared.

. . .

When their scheduled meeting time finally arrived, Tuck had made up his mind. In the end, it was a no-brainer. He wanted the luscious Dr. Malloy, and he was going to pull out all the stops to get her. If she didn't want him just as bad then he'd probably embarrass himself in the process, but those were the breaks.

And if she did want him just as bad, and he lost himself in her? Well, he'd cross that bridge when he came to it.

The only question now was how to get her to see him for what he truly was without making her suspicious. He had to transition from nerdy colleague to potential lover, and that transition needed to be smooth enough that it didn't make her think too hard about it. If he moved too fast, she'd think he was a phony, one way or another.

Today would be casual. No hard sell. They'd do the experiments, and he'd try to feel her out a little. He had something set up on the back burner that would test the boundaries, but he'd see how things played out before he committed to it totally. All the bases were covered, and he was feeling pretty good about the afternoon ahead.

When the day came to an end, he'd see if maybe she wanted to get a drink that night.

Yup, playing it cool was the way to go. He straightened the papers on his desk and glanced at the clock. Maybe she'd decided to ba—

A sharp rap on the frosted glass of the lab door interrupted his thoughts, sending his pulse tripping. No backing out for Dr. Malloy. At least he'd managed to map out some sort of plan before she'd gotten there. Now if only he could pull it off.

He took a deep breath and swung the door open, but the greeting on his lips died a fast death as he nearly swallowed his tongue.

Cricket stood in the doorway dressed in a pair of denim shorts and a white tank top. Thin sandals capped off firm, lightly tanned legs. Her toes were painted red, and in that instant, he became a foot man. Her hair was in a loose knot on the top of her head and the desire to release it almost brought him low.

She cleared her throat, and he realized he was gaping at her, hadn't said hello, and was blocking her path to get into the lab.

He stood back, waving her in with a sheepish smile. "I'm so sorry. I just never saw you dressed like that before. You look young enough to go to school here. How old are you, anyway?"

Oh, yeah. Real smooth. Maybe ask her weight next.

She chuckled at the obvious faux pas. "I'm twenty-eight. I'll take that as a compliment. Since I have to dress for work during the week, I like to keep it loose and casual on the weekends if I can help it."

He was still so poleaxed by her appearance, he couldn't respond. Great. Just when he'd decided to let her see how cool he was, all his cool melted in the face of her ridiculous hotness.

She stepped in, and he closed the door behind her, biting back a groan as he got a full-length shot of the back view. The faded denim clung to her curvy hips, the worn material cupping her round ass like…well, like *he* wanted to do.

He squeezed his eyes shut and tried to will away the erection that was rising, but it only made him more aware of the light, citrusy scent she wore.

"Are you okay? You look like you're in pain."

He opened his eyes to find her staring at him with concern. *Get your head in the game, jackass.*

"No. Nope, just a little bit of a headache. Would you like a bottled water? I'd offer you some coffee or soda, but I don't want caffeine to skew any results."

"Water will be fine, thanks."

He led her into the tiny office behind the lab and tried not to look at her as he got their drinks from the small fridge.

It was going to be a long day.

He led them back into the large lab area, then picked up the two spreadsheets that lay on the long Formica table and handed her one.

"Okay, so here's a list of the different foods we'll be trying. Then I thought we'd try aural stimuli. Last, some visuals. I had hoped to do scents as well, but we don't have the equipment we need to diffuse the scents enough to test more than one in this room." He met her gaze directly and made sure his tone conveyed his sincerity. "Anything you're not comfortable with, just let me know, and we'll skip it."

"Not much makes me feel uncomfortable about sexuality. It's the most natural thing in the world. I don't really get why people make such a stink. It's like being embarrassed of hunger or thirst." Her wide, dark gaze met his, and he sucked in a deep breath, nodding. "Still, it was great of you to do this. Way better than just joining the lessons. The kids will really respond to the fact that we went the extra mile and did a project, too."

"Agreed."

She glanced at her printout and scanned the contents as he rattled off the highlights.

"Okay, so we're going to measure the results three different ways, depending on the test. Pupil dilation, heart rate, and electrodermal response. I'm going to ask you to wear this galvactivator on your hand."

"Amazing little thing, isn't it?" she murmured, reaching out to touch the purple fingerless glove he held in his hand.

He nodded his agreement. She'd gotten it on loan from a university in Philadelphia. Tuck had been blown away when she'd told him about it. The glove stretched, fitting tightly to any hand, and could measure even the slightest increase of skin conductance. Since human skin became a better conductor of electricity during arousal, the blip in the body's normal behavior would be picked up by the sensors, and the light embedded in the glove would glow. It was a painless and easily measurable way to gather data. And it was a foolproof desire detector.

He couldn't wait to see it in action, but not because of its research potential. All he cared about was how the aphrodisiacs affected this particular subject. He tried not to think of what would happen when they switched roles.

Because if Cricket Malloy was within fifty feet of him, his glove was going to be glowing like a motherfucker.

• • •

It took a few seconds to adjust to the total darkness. Cricket took a steadying breath. Being blindfolded was out of the ordinary in itself, but being blindfolded and hooked up to a bunch of sensors while rocking the Michael Jackson look was downright nerve-racking. She was like a beetle on its back.

Vulnerable with a capital *V*.

Tuck's silence wore on her already-stretched nerves, and she cleared her throat, just to make some sound. "Well, if you're going to reveal your true identity as the Westfield Snatcher, end the suspense and show me my cage." Her voice came out sounding tinny. She tried for a laugh so he'd know she was kidding.

Mostly.

"My true identity? Nope, you get what you see. Well, you get what you hear, in this case I guess. Good old Tucker Lamb." He sounded nervous as well, and that was strangely comforting. "Anyway, you're going to hear a click. That's just me turning on the video camera."

Recording had been her own suggestion, and it made sense. Having a record of the experiments made it possible to go back and review the material again in the event that any data were missed in real time.

"The first item is something you listed as a food you like but that isn't considered an aphrodisiac. I just want to get a baseline response so I can differentiate between food you enjoy and foods that elicit a sexual response."

She nodded. The sound of foil crumpling was followed by a scrape.

"Open," he instructed. The huskiness of his voice gave her pause, but she parted her lips a moment later.

She closed her mouth over the cool tines of a fork and encountered something cold and creamy. The fork slid from between her lips and she chewed. Crunchy, too. Coconut cream pie with graham cracker crust.

"Mmm…" she mumbled, savoring the flavors. Eating with a blindfold on was liberating. She could focus all her energy on the taste. "Please, sir, I want some more," she said, laying on a thick Cockney accent.

He let out a throaty chuckle that warmed her to the bone.

"I don't want you to fill up before we get through the rest of the stuff, but I'll put it in the fridge so you can eat the rest later."

"Brilliant. Okay, I'm ready, what's next?"

The shuffle of feet and then the sound of his soft breathing, close enough for her to hear.

"Open wide, then bite down."

The scent hit her first. *Chocolate.*

She parted her lips and in came something sweet, no fork. She closed her teeth over the smooth object and bit down. Cool, sweet-tart juice spurted onto her tongue, and she groaned.

Chocolate-covered strawberry.

She chewed slowly, letting the fine, dark confection melt in her mouth before she swallowed.

"Oh man, you sure know how to treat a girl."

A few seconds went by with no response.

"Tuck?"

Had he left her alone? Suddenly nervous, she reached a hand to the blindfold.

"Sorry, I — uh, I had to record the data." His voice was so thick her nipples tightened in response. She longed to tear the covering away from her eyes so she could see his expression. See if it was desire behind that dark, silky tone. The not knowing was at once frustrating and thrilling.

She wondered whether the glove was lit up, then shoved the thought aside and cleared her throat. "Next."

She opened her mouth without prompting this time and waited. Again, the feeling of being totally vulnerable overtook her, but she kept her lips parted.

The room was so quiet, she knew where he stood by his harsh breathing. What if, instead of feeding her, he leaned forward and kissed her? What if he ran his tongue over her bottom lip, then nipped her lightly before sinking into her completely?

She sensed his body moving nearer, the heat of him tempting her to press close. His scent washed over her, sandalwood and vanilla, the minty bite of mouthwash—

The cool steel of a spoon almost made her jerk back. Instead, she closed her mouth as silky smooth honey glided over her tongue and slid down her throat. Delicious.

She licked her lips to pick up any errant drops, and the air in the room shifted. Tuck's breathing quickened, and her stomach fluttered in response.

"Again," he murmured.

She froze, unsure of his meaning. Lick her lips again? Or…?

"Open again."

Ah, the experiment. She needed to get her head out of the gutter. Obviously Tuck was just in the zone, focused on the task and distracted as he recorded the results.

She opened again and waited. And again, the forbidden thrill of being at his mercy rippled through her.

If he wanted to, he could wrap a fist in her hair and guide her waiting mouth over his thick cock, over and over.

A rush of warmth pooled between her thighs and she shifted in her chair.

"Wider."

Her nipples grew even tighter as she obeyed his command.

She nodded but didn't reply as she anticipated his next move. God, what if he did it? She could almost feel his smooth length butting against her lips, demanding entry. She'd tease him at first if he let her, suckling on the head of his cock before drawing him deep—

A banana. She smelled it just as it touched her lips.

She bit down, then chewed, trying to ignore her irrational disappointment. Who in their right mind wanted a man to tell her he was going to feed her, then stick his dick in her mouth instead? She almost choked on the banana as she tried not to laugh at her own foolishness.

Tuck was a good guy. She needed to remember that.

And a nice, long session with her vibrator later would surely make tomorrow's experiments a little easier.

Chapter Three

Blood pulsed in Tuck's cock like a steady heartbeat. He'd jerked off less than two hours ago, yet he was one well-placed touch away from coming in his pants.

Feeding Cricket without touching her was the sweetest torture he could imagine. The low purrs she made deep in her throat when she liked something. The sight of her little pink tongue collecting honey from her lips. Hell, just looking at her blindfolded with her mouth open was enough to conjure up fantasies that would make a porn star blush.

Then the glove had lit up. It was like a horny beacon, challenging him to keep it alight. Beckoning him to rub a thumb over her nipples, which had visibly peaked under the cotton shirt. Begging him to find out if her pussy was wet between those suddenly restless legs.

What would she do if he slid his hand under those tiny shorts and dipped his fingers into her heat? Would she moan the way she had when he'd fed her the coconut cream pie?

His dick was like stone, and he groaned, eternally grateful that she'd left the room. She'd gone into the office to check her e-mail while he set up the second set of tests, and he'd needed the break like nobody's business. Hopefully this next round would be a little less intense for him because if not, he was in deep trouble.

He finished queuing up the audio, then sat down to look at the results of the food experiments. The most compelling thing about the readings was that, while some of the samples had elicited a visceral, sexual reaction, the responses had spiked highest during the time *between* bites.

Interesting.

"All set?" Cricket asked as she breezed back into the lab.

He shelved his jumbled thoughts and motioned to the chair in front of him. "Yup. Have a seat." He handed her a pair of headphones. "Aural's next, so you can put these over your ears."

She giggled, and he raised a questioning brow.

"Sorry, but if someone walked by and heard that, they'd definitely get the wrong idea."

He laughed in return, trying desperately to quash a mental image of giving *her* oral while her thighs were wrapped around *his* ears. Turning his back to her, he conjured Abba the Hutt again as he needlessly fiddled with the media player on his laptop.

"I'm going to be plugged into the same audio so I can monitor what you're hearing when the readings change. If you don't mind, I'd like to have you blindfolded for this one as well. I think it helps to shut everything else out and it'll make you feel less self-conscious."

"No problem. I'm comforted by the knowledge that the shoe will be on the other foot soon." She slid the blindfold on and leveled him with a lethal smile. "Do your worst, Professor."

If she only knew.

He put on the spare pair of headphones and hit play, pencil poised over his notepad.

The first clip was music. She'd given him a list of her favorite songs, and he'd chosen one to get a baseline reading.

The thumping bass of the Black Eyed Peas' "My Humps" poured from the speakers, and Tuck bit back a chuckle. Cricket's taste in music was as fun and unpredictable as she was. From Sade to the Dave Matthews, from Kanye to Florence + the Machine, she liked it all. And damn if that didn't charm him, just like everything else about her.

He was getting in over his head.

He watched as she shimmied to the beat, snapping her fingers, unabashedly singing along. Her full breasts jiggled beneath her tank top, and he swallowed a groan.

Oh yeah, he was definitely in over his head. Best thing to do was get her out of his system as fast as possible, then walk away. No promises. Just get in, do the job, and get out. Sort of like the old days. That gave him an uncomfortable twinge of guilt, and he refocused on the task at hand.

The music faded as he jotted down Cricket's vitals before the next clip came on. It was the sound of a bed creaking. He didn't take his eyes off her face as the creaking came faster and faster and low moans echoed over the headphones.

A woman's voice first, "Mmm…yeah."

A low gasp, then a man's growl.

Heavy breathing, erotic sighs. Bedsprings humming as

the soft noises built up speed. Cricket's chest rose and fell with the crescendo, the glove illuminating as she leaned forward in the chair expectantly.

He wanted nothing more than to kneel down, spread her legs, and lay his mouth on her so he could ease her need. Would she wrap her hands in his hair as she pressed his face deeper?

The sound faded, but the silence was broken by the pounding of his heart. He only hoped she couldn't hear it, too.

Cricket sat back and ran a trembling hand through her hair.

Music again, but this time R&B, slow and sexy. A male voice, smooth as the finest scotch, curled around them. Cricket swayed in time as he sang of long, hot nights and slow lovemaking.

At that moment, Tuck would have traded his left nut for a voice like that if it would make her sway that way for him.

The music faded to silence and reality hit. It was decision time. He paused with his finger over the mute button and then lowered his hand.

Fuck it.

It was a calculated risk, but he was willing to roll the dice.

He had a feasible explanation well-rehearsed if she balked. After all, why spend hours on the Internet trying to find a clip when he could just record one himself?

At the same time, this was the first step out of the friendly/colleague zone into the man/woman zone. It would be almost impossible to step back from here.

As his own voice poured from the headphones, he held his breath.

"I need to touch you, babe. Will you let me touch you?"

Cricket's body tensed as if she'd been flash-frozen on the spot. Tuck cringed. Okay, she obviously had recognized his voice. Now what would she do?

"Tell me how you like it, Cricket."

Cricket's nipples pebbled under his gaze, and the light on the glove glared brightly. His cock responded with a surge.

Oh, hell yeah.

But that was only the start. Dirty talk light. How she reacted to the rest remained to be seen.

"God, I want you so bad. Open your shirt for me. Yeah. Like that. Now spread those sweet thighs. I want to feel that wet pussy raining on my fingers."

She ran her tongue over her lips and Tuck got light-headed as his blood flooded to his cock.

"Can I put my mouth on you? I need to feel your clit on my tongue…suck you, open you up until you come apart in my hands. And before the tremors stop, I'm going to plunge my cock into you. In and out, thrusting deep. Real deep. Legs shaking, hearts pounding. Mmmm… Over and over until we're sliding against each other, covered in sweat, ready to explode. Do you want that?" His recorded voice dropped to an intimate whisper. *"Do you?"*

The sound died away, which only made her soft response seem that much louder.

"Yesss."

Yesss.

• • •

Cricket reached a shaking hand to her headphones and

pulled them off. Her cheeks burned as she yanked down the blindfold.

Words tumbled out in a rush. "Can we take a break? I need to go the ladies' room."

She didn't meet his gaze or wait for his answer as she hightailed it out of the lab and down the hallway to the faculty bathroom.

She shut the door behind her and moved to the row of sinks. Using the cool porcelain for support, she turned on the water. As she bent to wash her face, she caught her reflection in the mirror and paused.

Holy crap.

Her cheeks were flushed, her hair was slipping from its confines, and her nipples were spiked beneath her shirt. She looked freshly fucked.

She filled her hands with icy water and splashed her face and neck. The water was cold enough to make her gasp, and that was good. Maybe it would give her the jolt back to Realityville that she so desperately needed.

This project was supposed to be fun and informative, not grindingly sexy and embarrassing. If anyone was supposed to be thrown out of their comfort zone, it was Tuck.

Tuck.

Her coworker, for cripe's sake.

She dried her face with a coarse paper towel and contemplated the man down the hall. What in the world was going on with him? The man she thought she knew, at least a little, was so not the type to say, "*I want to feel that wet pussy raining on my fingers.*"

Her stomach clenched hard. God, that had been hot. The whole thing was hot. Her cheeks warmed again, so she shifted focus.

Okay, what was done was done. They'd completed all but one of the tests and she'd gotten turned on. Big deal. That was the point of their research, so her humiliation was unfounded.

Sex was healthy, she reminded herself. Feeling sexy was one of the greatest things about being human.

She just hadn't expected to get quite that worked up. And she certainly hadn't expected it would be Tuck and not the aphrodisiacs doing the working. It had been a total surprise. Now that she had a handle on it, she'd be fine. She just needed a little breathing room to reassess things.

There was no question he'd known she was aroused. Even if her body hadn't betrayed her visibly, he had the data right in front of him. There was no point in pretending otherwise. As long as he didn't know it was *him* she wanted, there was nothing to be embarrassed about.

She'd just go back out there, make a joke and pray he hadn't heard her whispered admission. Or if he had, that he had the good grace not to mention it. Then she'd tell him she'd gotten a call and had to leave. They could pick up the rest of this another day.

She wasn't chickening out, she reassured herself. She was just taking a breather from boldness. *Tune in next week for our regularly scheduled programming.*

Yep, a couple days and it would all be fine. Except the videotape. That wasn't fine. She could've kicked herself. Her and her big ideas. But it was done and she'd just have to hope he didn't look at it. Or at least not until this whole thing was over and they had gone back to nothing more than trading salutations in the staff lounge.

She didn't stop to explore why that thought caused a twinge in her stomach. But as she shoved the door open and headed out to tell him she had to go, that little devil started yapping again.

Why should you be the only one off-kilter and suffering?

She paused in the hallway, staring at the laboratory door as if it were covered in scorpions. Hadn't she based her whole career on the idea that people shouldn't be ashamed of their sexuality? And here she was ready to scurry away just because of a pair of damp panties caused by a guy who was getting cuter by the second.

Not cool.

Shoving the door open, she took a steadying breath.

Time to give Professor Tucker Lamb a taste of his own medicine.

Chapter Four

"Ready?" Cricket called brightly as she sailed back into the lab.

She wanted to keep going. Tuck tried not to let the relief and exhilaration he was feeling show on his face. He'd been sure he'd pushed her too far and had been kicking himself since she'd walked out the door. Now though, he gave himself a mental high five. The risk just might pay off after all.

"Sure. Why don't you have a seat and we—"

"Oh, no," she said, sauntering his way with an extra swing in her hips that had him clenching his pencil so tight, it was a wonder he didn't snap it. "I think it's time to turn the tables. Tit for tat and all…"

Had she timed that phrase with a subtle jiggle of her breasts or was that just wishful thinking on his part? He eyed her and set down the pencil.

"Okay, I didn't know you had anything prepared for today." The plan had been for him to complete all the experiments on her first and then, once the results had been compiled a few days later, they would switch places. So what did she have in mind now?

"I don't have anything prepared, per se, but I'm down with improvising."

The words sizzled through him, but he tried to keep the reaction from showing on his face.

"I'm at your mercy." He tossed the pencil onto the lab table and held up both hands. "Where do you want me?"

She seemed to hesitate at that, and her gaze shifted restlessly around the room. "Um, why don't you sit there?" She motioned to the chair she'd been sitting in.

His imagination spun like a hamster wheel as he made his way over. She wasn't going to press him against the seat and straddle him because that would be ridiculous. And not unlike at least one of the fantasies he'd had about her in the past, he admitted ruefully.

At least he wasn't the only one who seemed uncomfortable, though. Cricket paced around the room, lips moving as though she was giving herself a mental pep talk. Either that, or she'd hidden the fact that she was batshit crazy this whole time and had finally decided to show it.

"Why don't you put the headphones on? I'll play some music so you're not distracted by outside influences, and we'll get some visuals together."

She sank into the chair behind his desk and clicked the mouse. His heart jacked up a little as sweat formed on his upper lip. Surely he wasn't stupid enough to have looked up anything important online at work? He'd been in the program for so long, covering his tracks had become pretty much second nature, so probably not. Still, a lifetime of hiding didn't lend itself to a whole lot of comfort when people were looking at your stuff.

"Just looking for some varying images. Should only take me a few more minutes."

He nodded, his heart and cock sinking a little as dreams of a lap dance died. Tugging the headphones tighter, he closed his eyes and concentrated on the music. It wasn't what he usually listened to, which tended to be more classic rock than anything, but it was bluesy and sexy and he totally got the appeal.

The cool touch of her soft hand on his wrist jarred him, and his eyes snapped open.

"Ready?" she mouthed.

He nodded and straightened. Game time. She held out her hand, and he followed suit, allowing her to tug the glove over his fingers. It was a tight fit, but it would do the job. Then he took time to say a silent prayer. *Dear God, please don't let this glove show her how much of a total perv I am by glowing every time she moves her lips. Amen.*

She turned and leaned over to retrieve a notebook and pen, and the glove glowed for a second as he stared at her shorts pulling tight over her ass.

He was so fucked.

He filled his head with thoughts of dancing mice, and the glow subsided before she faced him again. She turned his computer monitor his way and sat down next to it.

A blank screen met him, and he waited, whole body tense.

The first picture flickered into view, and he eyed it closely. A young woman, maybe twenty years old, riding a bicycle. She was attractive and her smile was pretty, but she didn't get his juices flowing, so he wasn't surprised when the glove stayed dark.

Cricket jotted something on her notebook and the next picture flashed across the screen, this one of a 1967 GTO. Poison green, restored to its original glory, and a serious piece of machinery. He chuckled, and some of the tension left his body. Okay, nice car, but that wasn't going to make anything light up.

She clicked the mouse again, and a new image took its place. This one he'd seen before. Scarlett Johansson as Black Widow crawling across the floor in a skintight, pitch-black suit. She looked hot. No question about it. And she had a body that reminded him very much of Dr. Malloy's. The glove glowed an eerie shade of lilac.

Cricket nodded, and a hint of a smile tugged at her lips as she scrawled with her pencil. If this had been as awkward for her as it was getting for him, he almost felt a little guilty.

Almost.

Then he remembered the way her cheeks flushed and her eyes had gotten all glassy and he could picture her nipples going hard under her thin shirt—

The glove went from lilac to violet in a nanosecond, and her eyes shot to his. The screen had gone blank, and his gaze was locked on her face. No explaining that away. Clearly he'd been turned on by her. Maybe it was time to get the lay of the land and see what was really up between them. Was this just flirtation on her end, or could this be the real deal?

He didn't look away, and her expressive eyes smiled back at him. When she finally turned back toward the computer, he was breathing hard. What now? Make a move or wait to see how things played out? The new Tuck would never make a full-court press for a girl like Cricket.

And sometimes the new Tuck acts like a pussy, his sub-conscious blared at him.

He was about to yank off the headphones and just come out with it. "I want you. I want to bend you over this fuck-ing table and drive my cock into you until you scream." But before he could open his mouth, she clicked the mouse and the next photo came up and the breath left his lungs in a whoosh.

What. The. Fuck.

The background music faded, overtaken by the sound of blood rushing in his ears. A naked woman in profile, built like a pinup, full, round breasts, nipples hard, head tossed back, long hair brushing the curve of her arched spine. Most of her face was obscured by shadows, but the rest of her was kissed by silvery moonlight. Hot damn.

His cock throbbed behind his zipper and he sucked in a lungful of air. He didn't have to look down to know the glove was practically neon. He stared at the picture harder, taking in the line of the woman's shoulder, the curve of her neck, the plump lips that—

He sat back hard enough that his chair wobbled as it hit him.

Cricket. The woman was Cricket.

Jesus Christ.

He dragged his attention from the most gorgeous pic-ture he'd ever laid eyes on and looked at the subject of it in real life. Her face glowed hot pink, and she bit her lip.

"Okay," she mouthed, and clicked the mouse, exiting out of the image viewer. He wanted to howl in protest. Beg her to blow that up into a poster and give it to him. But he did none of that. Because that wasn't how new Tuck behaved.

Instead he clenched his hands into fists, and sat there, waiting to see what she'd do next.

She ran a trembling hand through her hair and stood, motioning for him to take off the headphones.

"I've got to go. I just remembered…I have to pick up some groceries before the rush hour masses descend." She spared a glance at her watch and nodded, a little desperately, in his opinion. "Yeah, I've really got to go." She tore the page she'd been writing on out of his notebook and stuffed it into her pocket before wheeling around and heading for the door.

So much for getting the lay of the land. He was no closer to figuring her out than he'd been when they started.

The same couldn't be said a couple hours later. It was almost six o'clock by the time he closed the door to the lab behind him. He'd spent part of the afternoon going over the test results and the video trying to come to grips with his findings. Cricket may have rushed out a couple hours before with her awkward smile and flimsy excuse, but now he knew better for sure.

She was spooked.

He didn't blame her. He'd known exactly how attracted he was to her before today, and the intensity of it all had even spooked him. He'd gone into it thinking he was spending a day with the hottest woman he knew while he tortured himself with sexual fantasies. He couldn't imagine how *she* felt, since she'd come into it thinking she was in for an interesting day with a pleasant but boring colleague. She'd probably been hoping for a few laughs and some good data. Instead, she'd been hit between the eyes with a two-by-four.

Tuck tried to empathize, but couldn't seem to quash the

Cro-Magnon part of him that wanted to beat his chest in victory.

She wanted him. That was a verifiable, proven fact. He couldn't have hoped for better results than that.

Now he had to look deep inside himself and decide whether he wanted to try to close the deal for real. The internal debate didn't last long. All the usual bullshit reasons he'd stayed away this long rose to the surface: They were colleagues. He didn't want to ruin their working relationship. He wasn't in the market for anything serious. And, most importantly, he wasn't "that" guy anymore, and this could be a foot down the wrong path. A path of being led around by instinct instead of relying on his hard-won self-discipline.

Then, one thought — Cricket in that picture, naked in the shadows, lips parted, waiting — buried all the rest. At least the gravestone would read, "Here lies Tuck. Died happy."

Now that the decision to go for it was made, he had to figure out when. He weighed his options and decided sooner was better, so she didn't have time to talk herself out of him.

He mentally ran through all the possible scenarios from every angle before finally settling on a plan of action. He'd call and ask to swing by her house under the guise of dropping off a thank-you gift for all of her help. Wine was a good choice since she'd mentioned it in her food and drink preferences. Then he'd have to hope she asked him in to share.

Guilt pricked at him. Granted, he wasn't doing anything any other guy wouldn't do when he found a woman he was attracted to. But she didn't know him, the real him. She didn't know the things he had done and the man he had been. If she did, she would probably be running in the other direction.

He thought back to that afternoon and realized he felt more alive than he had in years, and wrong or right, he wasn't ready to give that up just yet.

By the time he cleaned up the lab and slid into the seat of his truck, he had practiced his speech a half dozen times. He dialed her number and waited for her to pick up.

"Hey." Cricket's soft voice flowed over the line like molasses, and his muscles tensed.

"Hey, yourself. Listen, are you going to be around for a while?" he asked, trying to keep his tone casual despite the fact that his heart was hammering hard enough to rattle his rib cage. "I picked up a little something for you as a thank-you for doing this with me, but I didn't have a chance to give it to you before —"

"Sorry about that. I feel like such a jerk. I'm always preaching about sexuality and how natural it is. Then I get a little damp in the panties during an experiment *about* getting damp in the panties, and I run away like a child."

She let out a shaky laugh and continued while Tuck tried to focus on the rest of her words, but he was firmly stuck on the "damp panties" portion of the show.

When he finally managed to tune back in, she was winding down.

"…over it now. And yeah, sure. I'm just hanging around anyway, so swing by. I'm at 356 Maple Way, across from the diner."

Two minutes later, he was on his way to Cricket's house. Just a guy stopping by to drop a gift off to a girl. No harm in it.

And that, ladies and gentlemen, is how you justify a load of bullshit.

. . .

"I have no moral opposition to one-night stands. I just think they're counterproductive," Cricket said, then took a deep sip from her glass.

"How so?"

When he'd arrived at her house, she had invited him in, cracking open the wine without any prodding at all. They'd been talking for almost two hours, and he was having the time of his life. She was funny, smart, and bawdy. It felt good just being around her.

Even in the short time they'd spent together, he was already picking up on little things about her. Like how when she was gearing up to make her point, she'd shrug beforehand, as if to say, "Listen, this is how it is," right before launching into a well-thought-out argument.

"A woman's sexuality is not at all like a man's. A man can literally fuck a watermelon and come. If you put enough friction on his cock, in some semblance of a rhythm, he will orgasm. It's a no-brainer." She shrugged again.

"But women," she said with a grin, "we're tricky. Some women need oral sex to climax, some need nipple stimulation. Some need to be on top and some on the bottom. Some like it rough, some like it nice and sweet. The odds that some random guy, in the course of one or two sexual sessions in a night, is going to figure it out are nil. Even if you have a woman comfortable enough with her sexuality to tell him how she likes it right out of the gate, it still takes fine-tuning. Not to mention the guys who are sensitive and take it personally. Then it can be ego-bruising and awkward to take direction."

She sat back with a smug smile and gave her closing argument. "Ergo, a woman soliciting a one-night stand because she's horny is tantamount to throwing a Rubik's Cube against the wall in order to solve it. Ain't going to happen. In fact, she's probably going to end up even worse off, all horned up from the petting. Better off investing the time with a guy who has a long-term interest in getting it right or just taking care of it herself."

She gave one final shrug.

He was torn between admiration and soul-deep desire. His whole body was tense, his cock like a rock. He wanted to respond but couldn't find his voice. That was probably a good thing, because he was afraid of what he might say. All he could think of at that moment was asking which type of woman *she* was. How *she* liked it. Unless he wanted to blow his chance—or worse, his load—he needed to stop picturing her in every one of those scintillating scenarios she'd mentioned.

Cricket stood and poured herself another glass of wine. "You know what would really help? If men started looking at it like a bank. The more you deposit, the more you can withdraw later. Make a woman come as a rule, she's going to be more receptive to regular sex and much more open-minded about what's on the table as far as experimenting. Common sense."

Common sense, indeed.

She looked at him expectantly, waiting to hear his thoughts on the topic. He cleared his throat and opened his mouth to tell her what an interesting theory that was. "Bullshit," he said.

Ah, Jesus, where did that come from?

"What?" Her eyes lit with interest and a hint of challenge.

He bit back his retraction and half-formed apology, allowing himself to think like the old Tuck for a minute.

"Well," he started off slowly, still framing his thoughts. "Let me clarify. The second half of your argument about the bank and making a woman orgasm is sound. But, with all due respect to your expertise in the field of human sexuality, that first part about one-night stands and the odds of a woman coming being nil? That sounds like a load of bullshit. Doctor."

"Care to back that statement up with an alternate theory, Professor Lamb?"

"Sure." He leaned forward on his elbows and looked straight into her eyes. "Your hypothetical woman just hasn't found the right guy for the job."

She tossed her head back and let out a whoop. Her uninhibited reaction brought an answering grin to his face.

"Oh, just like a man," she said through her laughter. "Don't you think most guys go into it with that mentality? That they're special, so phenomenal in bed, they're going to be the one to knock her socks off? Listen, I'm not downing your gender. I honestly believe most guys want to make a woman come. It's just that a one-night stand doesn't give him a sufficient amount of time to figure out how to do that."

"It does if he's paying attention."

Her nostrils flared lightly, and the smile slipped from her lips. "I already told you, most guys don't take well to being tol—"

"A man who takes a woman's pleasure seriously doesn't need to be told anything. It's all there. In the catch of her breath. The tension in her limbs. The way her back arches to press closer, to take more, her fingers fisting in his hair. The way her thighs tremble, then clench just a little tighter around his face when she…likes what he's doing." He lowered his voice to a whisper. "When her eyes get dark and she wets her lips."

Just. Like. That.

• • •

Blood rushed to her ears and a knot of heat flared low between her hips.

She lifted her glass to her lips and took a sip of wine to moisten her suddenly dry mouth before speaking. "In an ideal world, that's true," she acknowledged, pleased that her voice was strong and steady. "But to my mind, being that attuned to another person takes time and a concentrated commitment to the art of lovemaking that isn't present in the one-night-stand dynamic. After a night of drinking and prowling, you engage in mindless sex. The man is euphoric that he's getting laid, while typically, the woman is trying to fill an emotional void. He's focused on getting off, and oftentimes she's wishing she could rewind or fast-forward."

He nodded thoughtfully, sitting back in his chair.

Cricket took a steadying breath, at once grateful and disappointed that the tension had abated.

"Right, that may be true in a lot of cases, especially for people in their early twenties. But what about a woman and a man? Grown-ups who make a conscious decision to have sex for pleasure. Not because they're drunk or need a void filled. You don't think that happens?" Tuck met her gaze head-on.

Things had taken such an interesting and unexpected turn over the past twelve hours, she still felt like she hadn't caught up. It seemed that Tucker Lamb had a bit of big bad wolf in him. A shiver ran through her as she framed her response. "Yes. That does happen. And if you ask one hundred women over thirty if they've had an orgasm with a one-night stand under the conditions you describe, I bet you're looking at single-digit results."

Cricket wondered if it was the man, the wine, or the topic of conversation that was making her so giddy. She talked about sex a lot, so that wasn't it. She looked at her glass. One and a half glasses of chardonnay wouldn't faze her. She looked back at the man, and looked hard this time.

His hazel gaze held hers steadily. His lips quirked in a sexy half smile. He had a confidence about him that was decidedly out of step with the self-effacing, nonthreatening vibe he'd given off in the past. His shirt was pulled tight over wide shoulders, and she found herself wishing she could peek underneath.

"I accept that assessment," he said with a nod. "So we agree, then. There *is* a guy out there who can get the job done. You just haven't picked the right one yet."

"So we're talking about me now?"

He tipped his head in answer.

"Well then, we don't agree." She couldn't help but to try to push him as off-balance as she felt. "I'm a focused and giving lover, but I expect the same in return. It doesn't happen in a day."

He leaned back and grinned. "Okay."

"That's not you giving in, that's you patronizing me."

"We're at an impasse."

"Well, that won't do at all." She looked down at the table, at his strong, sure hands, and made her decision. The words just tumbled out. "Prove it."

His gaze snapped to hers, his hazel eyes growing dark.

She took a long sip of wine, then spoke again before her jangling nerves made her backtrack. "Put your money where your mouth is. I'm free for the rest of the night. You?"

His throat worked, and she bit back a smile. Apparently Professor Lamb wasn't immune after all. That was good, because somehow, over the course of the day, she had fallen head over heels in lust with him. If he won their little bet, she'd have spent the night with a good-looking, sweet guy and would sleep like a baby afterward. If he lost, she'd be able to put these feelings to rest and could always rely on her trusty pocket pal to take care of her needs. They were both adults. They had nothing to lose.

He stood quickly, moving faster than she would have thought him capable.

"I'm in." His hungry gaze ran the length of her, lingering on her breasts, her throat, her mouth. He held out his hand.

A quiver of anticipation ran through her and she struggled for composure. "Can you take direction without get—"

"No direction. If we do this, I'm going to play by my own rules. I postulated that a man who is paying attention to the physiological responses of a woman's body could and should make her orgasm. I stand by that. So, no verbal directives. That would be cheating."

Her nipples peaked. "And you?"

"And me what?"

"Do you get to come?"

"This experiment is about me proving my point. That's

enough for me."

Had his mouth always had such a sensual shape to it? She forced a laugh, but it came out sounding hollow.

"So I just have to sit there while you bend over backward trying to make me come? And I don't have to do anything at all?"

"Yup."

Her pulse went wild.

"Well, that seems like an offer I can't refuse."

"Good." His face was carved out of stone, so intense she wondered how she'd ever thought of him as puppylike. He held out a hand. "Come on."

She slipped her hand into his and stood. He didn't back up, and she found herself flush against him. He smelled delicious as she breathed him in, and her breasts brushed against his chest, her nipples pebbling at the contact.

His eyes narrowed and he shifted closer. He leaned low and for a breathless instant, she thought he would kiss her. His mouth stopped just a whisper from hers.

"Did I tell you how beautiful you are?"

She resisted the urge to close the space between them and wet her lips with the tip of her tongue. "No, but thank you."

He stepped back as if nothing had happened, then pushed her gently from the room. "I love looking at you dressed like that, but I want you to put on a skirt and heels. I'll be back in five minutes."

He wanted her to dress up for him? Hell, that was okay with her. She donned her favorite black mini and pumps, then reentered the living room, trying to quell the nerves jumbling her stomach. He still wasn't back.

She glanced out the window just in time to see him coming in from his truck, with his sports jacket on and a bouquet of tulips in his hand. As he made his way up the stone path, he smoothed his hair and checked his breath in a cupped palm. She grinned, her insides getting a little gooey.

He opened the door, flashing her a grin. "For you." He held out an arm. "Ready to go?"

"Uh, where? I thought…" They'd struck a bargain, hadn't they? Her cheeks burned. Had she misunderstood somehow? She frantically replayed their conversation in her head, eyeing her half-full wineglass on the table.

"What'd you think, I was just going to stretch you out on the bed and go to town?"

Actually…

He pinned her with his gaze. "This isn't amateur hour, Doctor. I'm old and wise enough to know that seduction begins long before you hit the bedroom. Now let's get out of here."

Chapter Five

Half an hour later, they were seated at Zuppa di Mare, the best seafood eatery in town. It was only a few blocks from her house, and the walk had been lovely. He'd held her hand the whole way, using his thumb to caress her wrist.

Their candlelit table was nestled in a little corner alcove, and smooth jazz played softly in the background. The place definitely catered to couples, and Tuck had scored the best seat in the house. He'd just ordered a bottle of champagne along with two orders of lobster sautéed in butter. While they waited for their food to arrive, they drank the bubbly and chatted. He listened attentively as she talked about her family, his attention never straying from her.

One more point for Tucker Lamb.

She took another sip of the icy, crisp champagne, then noticed he was watching her.

"Can I pull your chair closer?"

The husky tone in his voice triggered the memory of

another question he'd asked in that same tone.

"Can I put my mouth on you?"

Even the recording had almost made her knees buckle. She could only imagine what it would be like if he said it face to face in real life.

"Can I?"

She nodded dumbly, and he dragged her chair closer to his.

"Put your foot up." This time he sounded more commanding, and her heart stuttered before it resumed pounding.

A thrill coursed through her as she glanced around the room. Surely no one could see them. Besides, there was a long cloth covering the table. She slipped off her heel and laid her foot on the cool leather of the seat across from her.

A moment later, her foot was encased in his big, warm grasp. At first he just squeezed lightly as they chatted, but as the conversation wore on, he began to trace his finger lightly over her instep up to her sensitive ankle, then back down again. She bit back a sigh of pleasure. He shifted to lay her foot on his thigh before he made his way up her calf, tracing her muscles, making shapes on her skin.

"Why don't you come sit next to me?"

It wasn't a question. His gaze burned into hers. Her nipples drew tight as she imagined what he would do once more of her was within his reach. She didn't respond but stood to move beside him. He stood as well, shifting to allow her in.

She brushed past him and slid into the second large chair on his side of the table.

He sat beside her, laying his arm over the back of the seat, making small talk while absently caressing her shoulder. She tried to focus on what he was saying, but all she could think of was where he would touch her next. How far would he go here in public?

The waiter came back with their salads. As he placed hers on the table, Tuck's warm hand closed over her knee and squeezed. She shot him a glance, but he appeared to be totally engrossed in what the waiter was saying about seasonal vegetables.

"It looks great," Tuck said.

"Pepper?" the waiter asked her. She nodded.

Tuck's hand trailed from her knee, slowly up her skirt, inching up her thigh. He delved inward, running his hand over the soft skin on her inner thigh.

"That's good." Her voice was husky, and she cleared her throat.

The waiter ceased his pepper-cracking and Tuck waved him off.

"I was talking about you, not the pepper," she said to Tuck once the waiter was out of earshot.

"Yeah? I'm glad, but that's cheating." His tone was teasing and he didn't stop the caress. His hand moved a little higher, a little bolder.

"I'm not telling you anything you didn't know."

He bent his head to her ear. "Open."

Her whole body vibrated and she swallowed hard.

"Just a little, Cricket. Open those sleek thighs for me."

She sucked in a breath and scanned the room again. No one was even looking at them.

Slowly she relaxed her muscles, letting her legs fall open a few inches.

Tuck let out a hiss. He traced his fingers over her inner thigh, up and down, like he was painting her. Her body shook from the tension as she waited. One finger traced the very edge of her panty line.

"God, I can feel your heat. Are you hot there, Cricket? Is your pussy hot for me?"

A rush of wetness flooded her core at his words and drenched the small patch of cotton on her undies. Jesus, she'd thought he was shy?

She turned her head and whispered, "Yes."

His throat worked and his jaw tightened as he closed his eyes for an instant. "That's so nice to hear."

His movements were so slow and sinuous that she let out an audible gasp when he, quick as lightning, covered her pussy with his hand and squeezed. The pressure was too delicious, and a shock wave went from his hand to her heart and back again. She rode his palm, trying to ease the pressure building in her belly.

Her only focus was him, and she couldn't stop her shiver when he picked up his water glass and took a casual sip. His control was a turn-on. It fueled her desire as much as the hand massaging her clit through her underwear did. He stroked and pressed and stroked some more. Ah, what she wouldn't give to swing her leg over his thighs and ride him hard until the ache that was building swallowed her whole.

She closed her eyes and drew her legs together to savor his touch. Ready to let him—

"Oh, Cricket." He dislodged his hand and spoke low in her ear. "I want to win the bet, but not that easily."

She barely held back a groan. He was killing her.

He didn't look at her when he picked up his water again. He shot back the rest of the liquid before he shook the glass and dislodged an ice cube that slid neatly into his mouth.

Easing it from between his teeth, he held it between two fingers. "Let's put out some of that fire, then we can take our time building it back up again."

His eyes never left hers as his hand disappeared under the table. Her heart banged against her ribs as she strained, poised for his touch. When it finally came, she couldn't hold back the groan as she flexed her hips off the seat. The ice slid up the fiery skin of her thigh, then slipped beneath her underwear. He shifted to stroke it, long and slow, over her slit. Up and down, the frosty cube spread, pushing her beyond reason until he leaned over and gave her earlobe a sexy tug between his teeth.

With his mouth pressed to her ear, he murmured, "I can't wait until I can do this with my cock." Then pressed the remainder of the ice cube deep into her pussy with one long finger.

The combination of ice and fire made her buck. Her muscles clenched and spasmed, so close to completion she could almost taste it.

"Feels good, doesn't it? Feels good to me too." His nimble finger slid out, then back deep. Her body twitched, on the precipice.

"Again. Please, again."

He ignored her plea but his casual facade slipped for a moment as she felt the shudder run through him. She was desperate for release, and a flush of power overtook her when she realized that he was almost as affected as she was. Now to really even the playing field.

Without any warning, she reached out and covered his cock with her hand. He was thick and hard, his length pressed tight against the fly of his jeans. He froze and issued a muffled curse, halting the sensual assault between her legs.

She stared at Tuck's granite profile through lowered lashes as he struggled to maintain his cool. God, he was so fucking sexy.

Who the hell was this guy?

• • •

Tuck had been reduced to doing algebra equations in his head just to keep from embarrassing himself. Cricket's hot little hand had closed over him like she was getting ready to wrestle an alligator. Firm, tight grip, just like he liked it. He wanted to pump his hips up and down until he exploded.

Which, at this rate, wouldn't take long. Not the impression he was going for.

Regretfully, he pulled her hand from his aching cock. "We had a deal. We both know you can make me come. If that's what you want to do later, believe me, I'm not going to stop you. But right now I'm trying to focus on you. So let me do that, okay?"

She nodded and lifted her hand back onto the table.

He nearly wept at the loss. He risked a glance at her, then wished he hadn't. The pink cheeks, the parted lips, her ripe breasts rising and falling with each quick, shallow breath. If she was any hotter she'd burn the place to the ground.

He steeled himself, then dipped his finger into her molten heat again. His pulse thundered as he tried to quell the urge to take her over the edge right there…to fuck her with his finger until she screamed. Could she hear his heart pounding? Shit, who was he kidding? At this rate, he'd be lucky if she couldn't hear his *cock* pounding.

He shifted in his seat, trying to make room in his jeans, then slipped in a second finger. Her breath came out in a rush as her pussy clenched over him. Tight heat sucked at his fingers as he withdrew and began to rub her plump clit in slow, soft circles.

She panted, and blood rushed to his ears, mercifully blocking out the sexy sound before it drove him over the line between sanity and madness.

Like a slingshot, she jerked back. Her hand scrabbled at his, and she gripped his wrist. He stilled as he met her gaze, noting the panicked expression. A shadow fell across the tabletop as the waiter stood with dinner plates in hand.

"Here we are. Lobster sautéed in butter. One with broccoli, the other with asparagus."

He set the plates down and gave them a blank smile. "Anything else I can get for you?"

"No, thanks."

When they were alone again Cricket carefully straightened, retracting from his touch. He trailed a still-damp finger down her thigh before righting her skirt. He reached for his plate and pulled it closer, hoping like hell she wasn't furious with him for almost letting them get caught. He'd been so focused and in the moment, he hadn't even heard the server's approach.

"Looks good," he said, with forced enthusiasm.

"It does."

He dared a glance. Her eyes were still unfocused, glassy with need.

Excellent.

She took a gulp of champagne before pulling her plate close. She didn't pick up her fork. Instead she plucked a morsel of lobster meat, shiny with butter, between her thumb and forefinger. "You want?"

The husky rasp of her voice scraped over his frayed nerves, stretching his already-tenuous control even further. "Oh yeah."

She raised the meat to his mouth, and he took it gently from her fingers, sucking the salty butter from her skin.

"Mmm." Her low, purring moan made him want to press her back into her chair and take what he needed.

"Your turn." He pulled the most tender-looking chunk from the shallow dish and held it an inch from her mouth. She tipped her head toward him and ate from his hand, licking the butter from his thumb. Her full lips were shiny with it, and a single drop ran to her chin. She caught it with the tip of her tongue, and an image of her catching a drop of moisture from the head of his cock that way flashed through his mind.

How the hell was he going to make it through the rest of the meal?

Fuck it. He wasn't.

He'd taken a lot of risks so far with this woman, and they'd all paid off. He was going to roll the dice one more time. "Go to the ladies' room at the back of the restaurant."

Her startled eyes met his.

"*Now.*" He'd added a sharp edge to his voice and watched her response carefully.

The pulse in her throat fluttered, and she moved to stand. He kept his napkin over his lap as he rose to let her by. She didn't look back as she walked away.

Tuck waited a minute before he motioned to the waiter. "Can you bag this up? My wife's not feeling well." He slipped five twenties on the table before following the path Cricket had taken only minutes before.

He reached the entrance to the bathroom and paused before knocking softly. "Honey, feeling okay in there?"

A soft chuckle came from the other side, and he smiled. He opened the door and stepped in. Muzak echoed around him. There were five internal bathrooms, all empty save for one. He moved toward the closed door and pushed it open.

There she was. Cricket, standing in the stall, hair loose around her shoulders, eyes shining as she waited.

For him.

He shut the door behind him and faced her. "I have never wanted anything as much as I want you right now."

"Then take me," she murmured, standing on tiptoe to lean into him.

He slid his hands down to cup her ass, dragging her even closer. She gasped as his hard cock met her soft belly.

He started to speak but trailed off as she tipped her head to nip his chin...trailing her lips down to the pulse beating like a jackhammer in his neck. His skin sizzled at the touch, and he growled low in his throat. "Uh-uh. This is supposed to be about you, Cricket."

He pressed her until she stood on flat feet, then grasped her slim wrists in one hand, holding them above her head. He stepped forward, pinning her to the wall. Stealing under her blouse, he caressed the skin of her stomach and slowly moved upward. She moaned and arched her back, straining toward him.

With one finger, he traced the very edge of her lacy bra, and she groaned. "Come on, Tuck, please."

He covered her full, straining breast, flicking the hard

nipple with his thumb. She stiffened, and his cock leaped at her response.

"I'm ready. I'm ready now," she said, sweet desperation coloring her voice.

She was right. They didn't have a lot of time in any case. He slid away from her breast, down her slightly rounded belly to her legs. When he reached the hem of her skirt, he flipped it up, then cupped her pussy. She writhed against his hand, begging him without words.

He complied, squeezing and kneading her. He gripped the satin underwear keeping him from her slick heat and yanked hard, pleased when they came away in his hand.

"I almost came in my pants at the table when I touched your pussy for the first time. You were so wet, so hot."

He plunged two fingers into her, and she cried out. Wet silk. He steeled himself against the sensation, trying to imagine something other than how it would feel working his cock. He pulled back and pressed his fingers deep again.

"Oh God. Jesus, Tuck. I'm going to come like this."

Blood rushed to his head, and he knew if she said another word he was going to explode. He lowered his head and covered her mouth with his as he finger-fucked her in earnest.

He swallowed her cries as she arched and pulsed against him, urging him on. Her movements became frantic, and her body stiffened.

The sound of the bathroom door opening echoed through the room.

Cricket struggled against his wrist, but he didn't let go. She tried to close her thighs, but he shoved them apart with his knee. The water began to run, the sound barely discernible over the music playing. The stalls were more like miniature, tiled rooms, with doors to the floor so no one had to know they were there, as long as they were quiet. Still, Cricket's panicked eyes met his, and he released her lips, pressing his close to her ear.

"Don't make me stop," he whispered. "I want to make you come here, with people standing right outside the door. They'll never know," he reassured her.

He paused as the door a few stalls down closed with a click. "Except maybe one guy. The one at the bar who watched you walk in here. Maybe he'll know. He's probably hard as a rock thinking about touching you the way I am right now."

She'd stopped struggling. He took that as a good sign and traced her slit with his finger, playing over her clit before thrusting deep again. She moaned and he kissed her, nipping her plump bottom lip before rubbing his tongue against hers. In and out, he fucked her with his fingers, plunging deeper and faster as her body tightened. Her back bowed taut, and she sucked his tongue hard as she worked her hips in time with his thrusts.

The bathroom door opened and closed and then everything stopped as Cricket snapped. His world became a pinprick, and she was the focus.

He swallowed her muffled scream as she crashed over him. His cock bucked in his pants, weeping and twitching as her pussy clenched tight over his fingers again and again. In the violence of her orgasm, she garnered the strength to break her wrists free of their imprisonment. She reached for his fly and yanked it open before he could even protest. She tore her mouth from his and took a long, shuddering breath.

"Jesus, you win. You fucking win. Now fuck me."

An instant later, her hot little hand closed over his swollen dick and he saw stars.

"Oh, that's nice," she hissed. "I can't wait to feel you inside me, Tuck. Fuck me."

He grabbed her greedy hand in his and held her still, trying with all his might not to pump his hips and regain the sweet friction. If she asked him again, he'd be lost.

"I can't." The words sounded guttural to his own ears, like they'd been dragged out of him. And they had.

She tilted her head, uncomprehending.

"No condom." He hadn't really thought he'd need one in the restaurant, so he'd left them in his glove compartment back at her house. Idiot. "They're in the truck."

Her confusion faded and was replaced with a sly smile. She pushed herself away from the wall and put a hand to his chest, pressing him back.

"Well we can't just leave you like that, can we? Allow me."

She dropped to her knees in front of him and without preamble, sucked him hard. His legs buckled and he groaned, trying to remain upright. Her mouth was on fire, her lips and tongue working him with enthusiasm.

He lifted a shaky hand to her hair and wrapped a length of the tawny mass in his fist. She looked up at him through slitted eyes and pulled him deep. The sensitive head of his cock bumped the soft tissue at the back of her throat before she sucked her cheeks in, creating a suction that was almost unbearable.

"Jesus, you're going to make me come," he groaned. He couldn't hold back, needing her to finish it. He closed his eyes against the onslaught and used her hair to guide her to take him all the way.

Her throat vibrated as she hummed her approval, and he bit back a roar. The pressure coiled low in his loins, and his balls pulled tight, ready to launch. She ran her tongue over the head of his cock and sucked one more time, and then it was over. He was coming hard, battering her throat as his cock jerked and pulsed. A rush of come spurted into her magic mouth in waves as she stroked him with her hand.

When it was finally over, his legs were weak, and he leaned hard against the stall. His breathing slowed, and he released her hair, caressing it gently before reaching for her hand. He helped her stand, and she met his gaze.

She gave him a tremulous smile before she spoke. "So are you sure you have condoms in your truck or do we need to go to the store?"

Chapter Six

As they stepped into the warm night air, Cricket tried to remember the last time she felt so good.

Years.

She snuggled closer to Tuck, and he smiled down at her. If he was enjoying their time together as much as she was, they might really have the start of something here. She was already tingly inside at the thought of the night ahead.

He was leading her through the crowd forming at the club next door to the restaurant when a booming voice called out.

"Mini-Mick Tucker? Holy shit."

Tuck slowed and an older, slight man ran up to them from the back of the line.

A broad grin spread over his wrinkled face. "Hey kiddo, it's been so long! Shit, we thought you was sleeping with the fishes."

Tuck's expression went flatter than a soufflé gone horribly

wrong. "Sorry, you got the wrong guy."

His eyes clouded as he shook his head. "Mick, come on, it's me, Uncle Skeet. You remember, your d—"

"Look, I said you have the wrong guy," Tuck muttered through bone-white lips.

The wiry little man's smile faltered and he stepped away. "Yeah, maybe. Okay." He eyeballed Cricket, then shifted his gaze back to Tuck. His troubled face cleared before he touched his finger to his nose. "Sorry to have bothered you. I thought you were somebody I used to know."

Tuck laid a firm hand on Cricket's shoulder and led her away from the club.

What the hell was that? Her instincts lit up like a Golden Girl's birthday cake and she struggled to put the pieces together.

They had walked a silent two blocks before she decided to face whatever it was head-on. She tried to keep her tone light. "That was weird, huh?"

"Yeah. I think he must have been drunk or something." Tuck's casual tone sounded forced, but she let it pass.

After another minute, he filled the silence with idle chatter about school and some papers he needed to grade. She listened with half an ear and responded when it was required, but her mind was elsewhere.

Her mind was on Mick Tucker.

• • •

Tuck slid back into the driver's seat and slammed the door. He slumped forward, resting his head on the wheel. He tried not to picture Cricket's face when he told her he wasn't feeling well. Disappointed but resigned. He was disappointing her already.

What were the fucking odds, though? Two hundred miles from New York City and he runs into fucking Skeet McAllister. And not while he was alone. Oh, no. That would have been way too easy. It had to be when he was with Cricket.

Nausea roiled in his stomach as he tried to sort his thoughts. In his peripheral vision, he could see the light in her living room click on. It wouldn't do for her to look out the window and see him still parked there. The last thing he needed to do was add to her suspicions. He sat back and started the truck, then pulled away from the curb.

His mind was reeling.

Focus.

Okay, so what to do first? He needed to call Samuels and tell him. And then what? Move? Start over?

Not what he wanted. But this was bad. Really bad. It would have been different if some guy thought he knew him and said, "Hey, Bob Jones, right?" He might have been able to play that one off. He was nothing if not a good actor. But the fact that Skeet had called him out as Mick *Tucker*? That seemed downright shady. Not to mention his strange reaction. If his mind hadn't been addled with sex, he would have been able to think more quickly on his feet. And Cricket was way too sharp not to have noticed.

Fucking Samuels. He was all, "Witnesses are advised to keep their first names or initials when possible." Supposedly it jogged the memory or some nonsense. Tuck had tried to tell him he'd be fine using a totally made-up name. Shit, he'd been using them his whole life. But Samuels had persisted. Said it would keep him from making mistakes, not turning his head when called, or signing paperwork wrong.

Tuck had finally agreed, but he'd chosen to use his last name as his first name, going by the logic that he'd answer to it just as he had on the football field in high school. But at least he wouldn't be Mick anymore.

And more than anything, he hadn't wanted to be Mick anymore.

He smashed his hand against the wheel and let out a string of curses.

• • •

Cricket sat in front of her computer and swallowed the bile that rose to burn her throat. The newspaper headline leaped off the screen, the bold, black print in stark relief against the harsh white background.

CAREER CONFIDENCE MAN MICK "THE MICK" TUCKER MURDERED BY THE MOB

THE VERDICT IS IN. JIMMY "THE FACE" MANCINI HAS BEEN CONVICTED OF FIRST-DEGREE MURDER IN THE CASE OF THE STATE V. MANCINI. THIS IS EXPECTED TO BE THE FIRST OF MANY TRIALS AS MANCINI IS JUST ONE OF FOUR MEN SUSPECTED OF INVOLVEMENT IN THE PREMEDITATED MURDER OF MICK TUCKER.

THIS WAS A HUGE WIN FOR THE NEW YORK CITY DISTRICT ATTORNEY'S OFFICE AS IT REPRESENTS THE FIRST MAJOR VICTORY IN THE WAR AGAINST THE MANCINI CRIME FAMILY. THE ALLEGED DON OF THE FAMILY, JIMMY MANCINI FACES UP TO EIGHTY YEARS FOR HIS CRIMES, WHICH INCLUDE RACKETEERING, CONSPIRACY TO COMMIT MURDER, AND TWELVE OTHER CHARGES.

THE KEY WITNESS FOR THE PROSECUTION WAS MICK'S SON,

MICK JR. ONLY EIGHTEEN AT THE TIME OF THE MURDER, THE YOUNGER TUCKER HAD ALLEGEDLY BEEN HIS FATHER'S ACCOMPLICE SINCE HE WAS A CHILD. UNSUBSTANTIATED REPORTS FROM SEVERAL OF THE MICK'S SELF-PROCLAIMED COLLEAGUES WHO SPOKE UNDER THE GUARANTEE OF ANONYMITY CLAIM THE BOY WAS A KEY PLAYER AND WAS ORCHESTRATING ELABORATE CONS BY THE AGE OF EIGHT.

WHILE JUVENILE FILES ARE SEALED, ACCORDING TO REPORTS, MICK JR. ALLEGEDLY SPENT SOME OF HIS FORMATIVE YEARS IN ROCKLAND HOME FOR TROUBLED YOUTH, USUALLY COINCIDING WITH THE TIMES HIS FATHER WAS IN PRISON.

DESPITE HIS ROCKY RELATIONSHIP WITH THE LAW, TUCKER HELD UP WELL ON THE STAND. HIS EMOTIONAL TESTIMONY, INCLUDING HIS ACCOUNT OF THE BRUTAL KILLING, CLEARLY AFFECTED THE JURORS. IN SPITE OF THE DISTRICT ATTORNEY'S ATTEMPTS TO PERSUADE HIM TO MOVE DIRECTLY FROM PROTECTIVE CUSTODY INTO THE WITNESS PROTECTION PROGRAM AFTER THE TRIAL, TUCKER DECLINED, OPTING TO RETURN TO HIS FAMILY HOME.

The screen blurred, and Cricket closed her laptop with a snap, eyes burning with unshed tears. She refused to embrace her instinctive horror at Tuck's upbringing. If she allowed herself to examine that and really think of what he'd been through, she would fall apart.

She needed to focus on his actions and the choices he'd made as a grown man. And from where she was sitting, it sure seemed like the apple had fallen right next to the tree. According to the article, he hadn't gone into witness protection.

So why was he living under a different name? Her stomach cramped as she mentally ran through the possibilities. Was this whole "professor" thing just another elaborate con of some kind? And worse, was he putting their students in danger?

He'd duped the university into thinking he was a professor, duped the students, and, no matter how she turned it and as much as it made her face burn with shame, the fact was that he'd duped her, too. He'd pretended to be this nice, unassuming guy. Then when he'd had the opening, he made his move. And she was so stupid, she'd made it easy for him. Cricket Malloy, the perfect mark.

She should have known better. Only a bad boy could make her feel that good. She was so dysfunctional, she could pick them even if they were in disguise.

What had she gotten herself into?

• • •

Tuck stared at the letters on her office door.

Dr. Eleanor Malloy, PhD

It had been two days, and he still hadn't been able to make himself call her. But it wasn't about what was comfortable for him right now. She had the right to know the truth, straight from him. But if he told her, why would she ever want to be with him again?

She wouldn't. A lump lodged in his throat and he swallowed hard. And it didn't matter, she still needed to know. He wasn't that guy anymore. The guy who spoke more lies than truths. The guy who took and took and never gave. The guy who shattered people's dreams for profit and a thrill.

That guy was dead and gone, sharing a grave with the man who created him.

His temples pounded, and he tried to hold back the flood of bitterness and sadness that warred inside of him every time he thought of The Mick.

"Okay, boyo. Ya ready? Yeah? Good lad. Let's go over it one more time. What's yer name?"

He pinched the bridge of his nose between his thumb and forefinger and blocked out the voice ringing in his head.

Then he mustered the courage to bring his fist down and rap on the wooden door. Cricket opened it a few endless seconds later. She looked like shit. The skin under her eyes was thin and bruised. Her cheeks were almost devoid of color.

He was too late.

"Just tell me, Tuck." Her throat worked as she swallowed hard. "Is it just me you fooled? Are you even a real professor?"

His mouth worked, but he couldn't make the words come.

Her voice grew shrill. "Goddammit, these are people's lives you're screwing with. I can accept that you used me. I cannot accept you using this school and these students."

As much as he deserved her anger and mistrust, her words rained down on him like razor blades.

"You realize, of course, I have no choice but to report you to the dean. I have an appointment with him in thirty minutes."

Tuck didn't respond as nausea threatened. He handed her the sheaf of papers clutched in his hand, turned on his heel, and walked out.

• • •

Cricket lay on her living room floor, scattered paper surrounding her, as it all sank in. Tuck's note had been bad enough, but the clippings and the newspaper articles had made it so much worse. Speculation on crime after crime, all linked to his father. Then a few more after his father's death, with speculation that Tuck was following in his footsteps. But he hadn't done it for long. Because in spite of his refusal, something had finally clicked in him, and he'd entered the witness protection program six months after the trial.

She looked down and read the last couple paragraphs of the letter one more time.

I didn't go into the program because I was afraid of the mob. With Mancini out of the picture, things unraveled fast, and I don't think anyone was even looking for me. I did it because I was ashamed of myself. Ashamed of everything my dad and I had done. I wanted to start fresh with a new name, and a new life. One without all the grime on it. One I could be proud of. But my past is something I will never truly be able to outrun. And even after I started over, I pretended to be someone I'm not, then tricked you into being with me. Because deep down I guess I'm still that same guy who will do anything to get what he wants. And I wanted you so bad. Even worse? I wouldn't take it back, because being with you is the most honest thing I've done in almost eleven years. I only wish I deserved to know you and have you in my life.

— Tuck

She pressed her hand over lips and jumped to her feet. He wasn't getting off that easy.

By the time she got to his house, her stomach felt like a net full of butterflies. She knocked on the door and waited. The sound of footsteps creaked closer, and she steeled herself as the door opened. Tuck didn't even have time to open his mouth before the words poured out of her in a rush. "If you did something when you were a kid that you can't forgive yourself for yet, I can understand that. Everyone has regrets. But if you changed your life after all you've been through, then that counts for something, Tuck."

He held her gaze with haunted eyes but didn't step back to let her in. He hadn't shut the door on her, so she was going to take that as a sign of encouragement. She laid her hand on his chest and swallowed hard.

"Are you a real professor?"

He drew back as though he'd been burned, and his eyes looked sad when he nodded. "Of course I am. I—"

"And you care about your students?" She waited, her own heart pounding as loud as the one beneath her fingertips.

"Very much. This job is my life now."

"Then what's so unforgivable? If you're saying we can't even give this a chance because you somehow coerced me to be with you? Don't flatter yourself." She forced a laugh and stepped in closer. "You may have been good at the con back in the day, but I reeled you in as much as you reeled me in. Now you owe me a night, Tucker Lamb, and I'm going to have it. If you want me to go in the morning, I won't bother you again."

She held her breath as she waited for his response. A long moment passed, and her stomach churned as she thought he might refuse her. And then…

"Are you sure?" he asked softly, with a shake of his head. "I've done some things that—"

"Who hasn't?" she broke in with an exasperated growl. "But you've got to forgive yourself for that and accept yourself for who you are now." She trailed her hand lower and let her breath fan his. "A good man who is also a bad boy."

She craned her neck upward to see his response, but he never spoke. Instead his eyes went dark and needy, and he reached out and slid his hand into the waistband of her shorts, using them to pull her into his living room before kicking the door shut behind him.

He was on her in an instant, unsnapping her cutoffs and shoving them roughly down her legs, stopping at the back of her knees to caress her lightly there before moving back up her body.

"Take this off," he growled as he grabbed the neck of her T-shirt with both hands and pulled it over her head, baring her to his heated gaze. She hadn't taken the time to put on a bra, so she stood before him naked but for her underwear.

"God, your tits are gorgeous." He groaned as if he were in pain.

He wrapped a fist in her long hair and pulled, turning her head hard to one side. He bit her neck as he parted her legs with his hand.

He backed her up until her legs pressed against the soft velvet of the couch and she sat. With slow deliberation, he hooked a finger on either side of her underwear and dragged them down over her legs. He tossed them aside and faced her, staring down as if he'd been invited to enjoy his last meal.

· · ·

Cricket's sex glistened just inches from his mouth. He wanted to bury his face between her legs and drown in her. Instead he held back, teasing her, drawing it out. If this was the only time they had together, he wanted them both to remember it.

He closed his teeth on the flesh of her hip, then her thighs.

"What is it? Tell me what you want," he whispered.

"Please put your mouth on me."

He bent low and covered her with his tongue, lapping, then sucking. She cried out as she moved against his mouth. He quickened the pace, sucking harder, faster.

Her body stiffened, and he waited for her to shatter. Instead, she jerked away from him and sat up. She reached between them and grabbed his cock through his jeans and squeezed.

"I need to touch you, too."

"I can't take it," he rasped. But he stood and thrust his jeans off. He pressed her back, positioning himself between her legs. He halted and let out a vicious curse.

"I'll be right back. No condom."

She reached down to pick up her shorts and a row of five unfurled in her hand.

"You're the smartest woman I've ever met."

She pulled him close, rubbing her breasts over his torso and stomach as he fumbled with the packet. He finally got it covered and she was there waiting, giving him a guided tour of her hot pussy. He slid into her an inch, then two, gritting his teeth in an effort not to thrust hard and fuck her like an animal. She would have none of it. She snapped her hips to his, taking him all in.

Her low gasp gave him pause, until she wriggled beneath him, urging him to move. He pulled back and plunged forward again, filling her, stretching her before backing away. Slow and steady, he rocked in and out, fanning the flames, drawing the anticipation out.

Then Cricket reached around and gripped his ass with both hands, pulling him into her until he was seated to the hilt. She ground against him furiously, her body knowing what it needed and taking it. His screamed for release in turn as her slick inner walls squeezed him. He matched her rhythm with long, deep strokes. They moved faster as he bent his head to lick and suck her nipple while he fucked her. That threw her over the edge, and her body tensed, tightening around him.

A keening wail built in her throat, then she shattered, convulsing around him. Shudders racked her body as she worked her clutching pussy over his cock. It was like a fist, pulling at him relentlessly until a second later he tumbled after her. He flexed deep, groaning her name as he exploded.

• • •

She didn't know how long they slept, wrapped in each other on his couch, but when she woke up, it was dark. Her leg was numb, and she tried to extract herself from his hold without waking him.

"Trying to escape?" he asked, his voice husky and warm.

"Nope. Just trying to avoid the need for amputation is all."

He laughed. "Sorry about that."

Standing, he held out a hand to help her up.

She tried not to drool as she took in the sight of his naked body in the moonlight. His shoulders were wide, his chest tapering down to chiseled abs and lean hips. Her pulse skittered.

"Damn. Professor Lamb, you got it going on. You had way too many clothes on at the restaurant, and I only got to see bits and pieces earlier. Me likey."

He waggled his brows playfully. "You're not so bad yourself."

The softness in his eyes caught her, and she faced him straight. "I like you, Tuck. And I want to see where this goes."

"I want that, too." His face looked troubled. "But what if someone else finds out? Skeet will keep it hush-hush, and Mancini died in a prison fight last year, so I don't think your safety is a concern, but it's a small world. What if someone finds out? The school wouldn't want that kind of publicity. I'd have to leave, start over again." His soulful hazel eyes searched hers. "What if I can't give you up then?"

She shrugged and shook her head slowly. Who knew exactly what the future held? All she could say for sure was that she was willing to gamble on him. "Hopefully that won't happen. But if it does and you can't give me up by then, it'll be because we're meant to be, and I'll go with you."

"That sounds real good." He nodded and brushed her hair away from her forehead. "I know what you said, and I know you aren't mad, but I want to make sure I say this. I'm sorry I couldn't tell you the truth right from the start. But I really am different. I've been a good man. I want to continue to be a good man." He gazed at her in earnest, and she caressed his cheek.

"I believe that. As long as you keep some of the bad boy, too. I like you a little bad, Tuck," she murmured.

The serious expression gave way to a killer grin. "Well, now that you mention it, I was thinking, we have two more weeks before the projects are due. We can go to the lab and pick up the glove and maybe some whipped cream, finish those experiments…"

She laughed and pressed her mouth to his. Oh yeah, this was definitely worth a shot.

About the Author

Christine Bell is one half of the happiest couple in the world. She and her handsome hubby currently reside in Pennsylvania with a four-pack of teenage boys and their two dogs, Gimli and Pug. She doesn't like root beer, clowns or bugs (except ladybugs, on account of their cute outfits), but lurrves chocolate, going to the movies, the New York Giants and playing Texas Hold 'Em. Writing is her passion, but if she had to pick another occupation, she would be a pirate... or, like, a ninja maybe. She loves writing fun and adventure-filled romance stories, but also hopes to one day publish something her dad can read without wanting to dig his eyes out with rusty spoons. Christine also writes erotic romance under the pen name Chloe Cole and YA fiction as Christine O'Neil.

Christine loves to hear from readers, so please feel free to get in touch with her via her website www.christine-bell.com

Also by Christine Bell...

LITTLE WHITE LIE

REFORMING THE ROCK STAR

HOLDING OUT FOR A HERO

Dare Me series

DOWN AND DIRTY

DOWN FOR THE COUNT

DOWN THE AISLE

DOWN ON HER KNEES

Perfectly Matched series

DIRTY TRICK

DIRTY DEAL

For Hire series

WIFE FOR HIRE

GUARDIAN FOR HIRE

www.ingramcontent.com/pod-product-compliance
Lightning Source LLC
Chambersburg PA
CBHW050834180626
46814CB00004B/1610